story rhyme

illustrations by Elizabeth Wilson

© Copyright Three Four Five Limited 1972

S.B.N. 903016 08 7

First published in Great Britain 1972 by THREE FOUR FIVE LIMITED, 92a Old Street, London, E.C.1.
Printed by Oxley Press Limited, Nottingham, England
Distributed by KIDDICRAFT LIMITED, Kenley, Surrey.
Made in Great Britain.

Everyone needs a well trained memory. Accumulative stories are a valuable aid in helping children develop their powers to remember and retain information. There are many folk tales and fairy stories which accumulate characters or events as the story progresses. To name a few there is 'Chicken Licken', 'The Gingerbread Man', 'The Pig Who Wouldn't Go Over The Stile' and 'The Golden Goose'. Perhaps the best loved of all such stories is 'The House That Jack Built'. The rhymes and constant repetition help children remember the sequences of the story.

Teachers of speech always enthuse about this ancient story. The vowel sounds are emphatic and the word endings have sharp consonants. Therefore, children reciting this narrative rhyme are practising fluent speech.

Related Ideas

Children will discover from this story that one event leads to another and one character relates to another. The idea of sequences is an interesting one for children to examine. Young children begin to know that their actions can affect other people. Most children have experienced, for example, the effect of leaving a toy in a dangerous place. The child leaves the toy in the kitchen doorway – a brother or sister trip over it – banging their head and breaking a beaker – mother clears up the mess – the dinner is burned – father comes home to find he has no dinner – mother is upset – the child goes to bed without a story! Of course, the same type of story can be told with a happy ending. For example, mother is very busy – the child helps her lay the table – father comes home from work and says "What a pleasant house to come home to".

Rhymes about 'Jack'

So many rhymes, stories and proverbs refer to a character called 'Jack'. Children might enjoy remembering some of them after they have played with this story. Among the best known are 'Jack and Jill', 'Jack Spratt', 'Jack be nimble', 'Little Jack Horner', 'When Jacky's a good boy, he shall have cakes and custard', 'Jack and the beanstalk', 'A Jack for every Jill' and 'Jack of all trades master of none'.

About the Record in this Book

The children singing, chanting and playing this story are aged between five and eleven. It is hoped that younger children will feel encouraged to join in with the slightly more mature voices. They will enjoy beating out the rhythm of the words with a simple percussion instrument. If there are no instruments available try some improvisations and let the child decide which he prefers. A yoghurt pot containing a few grains of rice or sugar (fix with silver foil over the top and secure with an elastic band), a coffee tin to beat with, a wooden spoon or two wooden building blocks to beat together.

Father Too!

A man's voice can be heard saying one verse of the story. This has been included, not only to give light and shade to the sound of the voices but, because fathers are so often excluded from the education of young children. Children love to hear fathers, as well as mothers, reading stories or singing rhymes with them. Perhaps the owner of this book will persuade father to read a verse or even two!

If your child enjoys this book you may be interested to know that there is a Three Four Five Nursery Course available.

This is a completely new method of pre-school education for the child aged three to five. It is a carefully planned, fully comprehensive course of nursery education mailed to your home in monthly instalments.

The course includes games, pictures, puzzles, stories, rhymes, colouring and modelling and the first steps towards number work, reading, writing and self expression.

Here are a few of the press comments about the course:—

". . . . Ingenious product should help fill the gap between the pressingly large demand for pre-school 'education' and the pathetically small supply."

The Spectator.

"What a change it makes when mothers who know what they're talking about go into business . . . just what house-bound mothers have been waiting for."

Sunday Mirror.

". . . . will disseminate information on developing a child in these important early years, apart from helping to cement the mother-child relationship."

The Guardian.

"Parents anxious to start teaching their children before they reach school age can sometimes do more harm than good with unimaginative lessons. Nursery Three Four Five is a colourful aid to mothers, to help children to play their way through the early stages of learning."

The Observer.

For full details, without any obligation to buy, write to the Circulation Manager, Three Four Five Ltd, 92a Old Street, London, E.C.1.

This is the house that Jack built.

This is the malt that lay in the house that Jack built.

This is the rat that ate the malt,
That lay in the house that Jack built.

This is the cat that killed the rat,
That ate the malt,
That lay in the house that Jack built.

This is the dog that worried the cat,
That killed the rat,
That ate the malt,
That lay in the house that Jack built.

This is the cow with the crumpled horn,
That tossed the dog,
That worried the cat,
That killed the rat,
That ate the malt,
That lay in the house that Jack built.

This is the maiden all forlorn,
That milked the cow with the crumpled horn,
That tossed the dog,
That worried the cat,
That killed the rat,
That ate the malt,
That lay in the house that Jack built.

This is the man all tattered and torn,
That kissed the maiden all forlorn,
That milked the cow with the crumpled horn,
That tossed the dog,
That worried the cat,
That killed the rat,
That ate the malt,
That lay in the house that Jack built.

This is the priest all shaven and shorn,
That married the man all tattered and torn,
That kissed the maiden all forlorn,
That milked the cow with the crumpled horn,
That tossed the dog,
That worried the cat,
That killed the rat,
That ate the malt,
That lay in the house that Jack built.

This is the cock that crowed in the morn,
That waked the priest all shaven and shorn,
That married the man all tattered and torn,
That kissed the maiden all forlorn,
That milked the cow with the crumpled horn,
That tossed the dog,
That worried the cat,
That killed the rat,
That ate the malt,
That lay in the house that Jack built.

This is the farmer sowing his corn,
That kept the cock that crowed in the morn,
That waked the priest all shaven and shorn,
That married the man all tattered and torn,
That kissed the maiden all forlorn,
That milked the cow with the crumpled horn,
That tossed the dog,
That worried the cat,
That killed the rat,
That ate the malt,
That lay in the house that Jack built.

farmer
cock
priest
man
maiden
cow
dog
cat
rat
malt
house